LISTENER'S GUIDE

In
CLASSICAL
mood

Expressions

of

Love

Expressions of Love

Throughout the history of classical music, no emotion has found richer expression among the great composers than love. While love, like music, comes in many forms, this volume of *In Classical Mood* is devoted to love's more tender side. From the openly romantic *Liebesträume* of Liszt to the yearning of Brahms's *Symphony No.3*, from the plaintive strings of Elgar's *Salut d'amour* to the emotional power of Rachmaninov's *Piano Concerto No.2*, *Expressions of Love* is sure to strike a tender chord in any heart.

THE LISTENER'S GUIDE — WHAT THE SYMBOLS MEAN

THE COMPOSERS
Their lives... their loves.. their legacies...

THE MUSIC
Explanation... analysis... interpretation...

THE INSPIRATION
How works of genius came to be written

THE BACKGROUND
People, places, and events linked to the music

© MCMXCVI IMP AB   In Classical Mood™   IMP AB, produced under license by IMP Inc.   Printed in China.   US P 2201 12 005

Contents

FRANZ LISZT *1811–1886*

Liebesträume No.3 in A-flat

This very famous and romantic *Liebesträume,* or "Dream of Love," for the piano opens in a mood of quiet and tender reflection. It builds up to a passionate climax, then fades away again on a note of soft and sweet remembrance. Franz Liszt also included some dazzling examples of his own virtuoso piano style without ever disturbing its basic dreamlike quality.

LISZT MANIA

Hungarian-born Liszt was one of the first piano virtuosos and the musical superstar of his day. As a young man he looked like a mythical god and played with ardent showmanship. He turned the piano sideways to his audience so that they wouldn't miss one note and could also admire his handsome profile! As a result, woman used to faint when he would play and fought over locks of his hair, buttons off his clothes, and even his cigar butts.

SHOWMAN AND VIRTUOSO

The great showman was only one side of Liszt. He soon tired of his celebrity lifestyle and retired to the peaceful old town of Weimar in Germany, where J.S. Bach had once been court organist. There, Liszt spent more time on serious composition (including his three *Liebesträume* nocturnes) and on promoting the music of some of his greatest musical contemporaries, including Berlioz and Wagner.

TURBULENT LOVE

Liszt wrote his three piano *Liebesträume* nocturnes from a depth of personal experience in matters of the heart. Among his many amorous affairs were those with a French countess, Marie d'Agoult, and a Polish princess, Carolyne Sayn-Wittgenstein, both of whom were already married when he met them. Among his other mistresses were the young courtesan Marie Duplessis, who was the original "Lady of the Camellias," and the notorious courtesan and dancer Lola Montes.

Above: *Liszt lived with Marie d'Agoult for four years; she bore him three children.*

Left: *Dancer Lola Montes was later the mistress of Ludwig I of Bavaria.*

KEY NOTES
Liszt made a number of piano transcriptions, or arrangements of music, from other composers' operas, including Wagner's great operatic love story, Tristan and Isolde, and works by Berlioz, Rossini, Schubert, and Tchaikovsky.

PYOTR TCHAIKOVSKY *1840–1893*

Romeo and Juliet

FANTASY OVERTURE

William Shakespeare's *Romeo and Juliet* is the tragic story of two young lovers caught up in the bitter feuding between their families, the Montagues and the Capulets. In this "fantasy-overture," Tchaikovsky evokes Romeo and Juliet's deep but doomed love for each other. The extract begins with their touching love theme. It is followed by a tender passage played on soft muted strings, before the theme returns on the flutes with a horn solo sounding behind them.

INSPIRATION TO MANY

The powerful love, passion, and tragedy of Shakespeare's play *Romeo and Juliet* has fascinated many composers besides Tchaikovsky. It inspired Bellini, Gounod, and Delius to create operas; Berlioz wrote a dramatic choral symphony; and Prokofiev composed a stunning ballet score.

KEY NOTES

Romeo and Juliet *was not the only piece that Tchaikovsky wrote based on one of Shakespeare's plays. He also composed two more symphonic fantasies based on* The Tempest *and* Hamlet.

GUSTAV HOLST *1874–1934*

The Planets
VENUS, THE BRINGER OF PEACE

Venus in this famously gentle piece expresses the cooler, more universal side of love, which explains the work's reference to her as "the Bringer of Peace." A soft but confident call on solo horn with answering chords high on the flutes instantly evoke a feeling of tenderness. Later, the sweet sound of solo violin enhances this mood. Meanwhile, rich orchestral harmonies and delicate chimes from the harp and celeste (a keyboard instrument) work together to create an unearthly atmosphere of love and peace.

THE PLANETS

Holst composed *The Planets* between 1914 and 1916. By the time he completed it, Europe was already ravaged by war. The inspiration for the suite came not from the planets of the solar system, but from astrology, in which Holst had a passing interest. The composer began by attaching his own subtitles to each planet, Venus being "the Bringer of Peace." Then, as Holst's daughter later wrote, he simply "let the music have its way with him." The other movements are: "Mars, the Bringer of War"; "Mercury, the Winged Messenger"; "Jupiter, the Bringer of Jollity"; "Saturn, the Bringer of Old Age"; "Uranus, the Magician"; and "Neptune, the Mystic."

The astrological significance of the planets, not the planets themselves, provided Holst with the inspiration for The Planets.

A FAMOUS PARTNERSHIP

The distinguished English conductor Sir Adrian Boult *(left)* was a great champion of the music of fellow countryman and composer Gustav Holst. It was Boult who conducted the first public performance of *The Planets* in London in 1920, and he later became the work's most celebrated interpreter. With Boult's help, *The Planets* soon made Holst famous worldwide. This came as a great surprise to the modest composer, who never considered it to be his best work.

TEACHING AND COMPOSING

Holst's family came from Sweden, but he was born in the elegant English spa town of Cheltenham and spent most of his life in London. To earn a living, he played the trombone, before becoming a music teacher at various London schools, notably St. Paul's Girls' School in Hammersmith. When composing, Holst worked in a soundproof room because the slightest noise disturbed him. Many of his interests influenced his work. For instance, with his friend and fellow composer Vaughan Williams, Holst traveled around England collecting old folk songs. He was also interested in Eastern mysticism and even taught himself to read the ancient Indian language of Sanskrit to learn about mythology, which inspired several of his later works.

Hammersmith Bridge, London, which Holst walked over daily on his way to his teaching job at St. Paul's Girls' School.

KEY NOTES

There is no movement in The Planets *dedicated to* Pluto. The reason for this is a simple one: This planet was only discovered in 1930, fourteen years after Holst had finished work on The Planets.

GEORGE GERSHWIN
1898–1937 arr. Heifetz

Porgy and Bess

BESS, YOU IS MY WOMAN NOW

*P*orgy and Bess is the story of a poor, crippled black man who lives on Catfish Row in Charleston, South Carolina. Despite his disabilities, Porgy has taken Bess away from a drunken and murderous stevedore, Crown. In this arrangement, we hear the melody to his aria, or song, "Bess, You Is My Woman Now." In the opera, Bess adds her voice to his, creating one of the most tender and poignant of all operatic love duets.

LEARNING A LESSON

In 1928, Gershwin, already a very successful and rich songwriter, asked French composer Maurice Ravel for some lessons in composition. It is said that Ravel asked Gershwin how much he earned from his music. When Gershwin told him, Ravel replied, "Then, Monsieur Gershwin, I think it is I who should take lessons from you!"

KEY NOTES

Jascha Heifetz (1899-1987), world famous violin virtuoso and friend and admirer of Gershwin, arranged a suite of melodies drawn from the opera Porgy and Bess, *including this piece for violin and piano.*

WOLFGANG AMADEUS MOZART
1756–1791

The Marriage of Figaro

VOI CHE SAPETE

Cherubino, a page boy in the household of Count Almaviva, is to be dressed up as Susanna, the Countess's maidservant, in order to lure the Count into an embarrassing situation. Though the part of Cherubino is that of a young man, it is played and sung by a soprano. In this famous aria, sung while he is being fitted in Susanna's clothes, Cherubino reflects on the joys and sorrows of love as seen through the eyes of an innocent teenager.

TROUSER ROLES

There is a long history in opera of women, both sopranos and contraltos, appearing in male roles. The traditional Italian name for this is *travesti*, or "trouser roles." Cherubino, the lovesick page boy in *The Marriage of Figaro*, is one of the most famous of all *travesti* roles.

KEY NOTES

Two other famous "trouser" roles are Prince Orlofsky in Johann Strauss II's Die Fledermaus, and Octavian, in Richard Strauss's opera Der Rosenkavalier, who is the ardent young lover of the Marschallin.

SIR EDWARD ELGAR
1857–1934

Salut d'amour

Sir Edward Elgar wrote *Salut d'amour*, or "Love's Greeting," the year before his marriage to Caroline Alice Roberts. Composed originally for the piano and then arranged for the orchestra, this simple yet moving piece speaks of love at its sweetest and most tender moment. This short piece creates an image of a man offering a bouquet of flowers to his true love as a sincere expression from his heart.

CATHOLIC FAITH

Elgar belonged to the Roman Catholic faith, which was unusual for an Englishman. He proudly proclaimed the fact in *The Dream of Gerontius*, which describes the progress of the soul after death. Elgar dedicated the work to the writer of the original poem, Cardinal Newman—the most celebrated English Catholic of his day.

UPS AND DOWNS

Sir Edward Elgar was considered one of England's all-time great composers. He was the son of an organist and teacher in the old cathedral city of Worcester. Through the years, he had a tough struggle gaining recognition as a serious composer. The work that finally brought him fame was his *Enigma Variations* for orchestra. Soon after, his *Pomp and Circumstance* marches turned him into a national hero. He was suddenly showered with honors and conducted his music around the world, including the United States. By the time of World War I, he became depressed, believing that he had outlived the age his music spoke for.

The Malvern Hills near Worcester (above), *which inspired Elgar's* (right) *imagination.*

THE MAKING OF HIM

Elgar was thirty-two years old and still almost unknown in the musical world when he married Caroline Alice Roberts, the daughter of a high-ranking British army officer. She proved to be both his inspiration and motivation. All his finest music was written during the years of their marriage. Unfortunately, after Alice died in 1920, Elgar wrote little more for the remaining fourteen years of his life.

KEY NOTES

As the son of an organist, Elgar learned to play the organ, as well as other instruments, in his youth. He managed to learn much about music on his own.

ENRIQUE GRANADOS
1867–1916

The Beauty and the Nightingale

The original title for this charming Spanish piece is *La maja y el ruisenor*. Its romantic theme conveys the enchanting but plaintive song of a delicate nightingale as it sings through the darkness of a clear night. This sweet mood is softly complemented by more voluptuous-sounding music. As the notes continue on, they breathe the warmth and fiery passion of Spain.

INSPIRED BY GOYA

The Beauty and the Nightingale comes from a group of piano pieces collectively called *Goyescas*. These pieces were inspired by the paintings of the great Spanish artist Francisco Goya *(above)*. Granados subsequently used these same works in an opera, also called *Goyescas*, in which a haughty Spanish beauty, Rosario, arouses the jealousy of her lover by flirting with a bullfighter. Eventually, Rosario provokes a duel in which the lover is killed. In the opera, she sings *The Beauty and the Nightingale* just before the fatal duel.

LOVE OF SPAIN

Like Smetana in Czechoslovakia and Grieg in Norway, Spanish composer Enrique Granados was a great nationalist, expressing his love of his homeland through his music. He studied with a distinguished Spanish musical scholar, Felipe Pedrell, learning from him much about old Spanish folk song and dance. His own compositions, including several operas, piano works and songs, overflow with the sound of traditional melodies and rhythms of Spain, especially his native Catalonia.

LOVE AND DEATH

It was Granados's love for his wife that led to his tragic death during the World War I at the age of forty-nine. He had given a recital at the White House that caused him to miss a boat which would have taken him straight home to Spain. Instead, he took a roundabout route via England and France. While crossing the English Channel, his boat the SS *Sussex* (*below*) was sunk by a German submarine. Granados was picked up by a lifeboat, but seeing his wife struggling in the sea, he jumped in to save her. Both drowned.

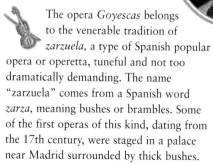

POPULAR OPERA

The opera *Goyescas* belongs to the venerable tradition of *zarzuela,* a type of Spanish popular opera or operetta, tuneful and not too dramatically demanding. The name "zarzuela" comes from a Spanish word *zarza,* meaning bushes or brambles. Some of the first operas of this kind, dating from the 17th century, were staged in a palace near Madrid surrounded by thick bushes.

K E Y   N O T E S

Another piece from **Goyescas** is El fandango del candil, or "Kitchen Fandango." Fandango is a lively Spanish or Spanish-American dance.

NIKOLAI RIMSKY-KORSAKOV
1844–1908

Scheherezade

THE YOUNG PRINCE AND THE YOUNG PRINCESS

In this romantic and exotic love story from *Arabian Nights*, the Prince first proclaims his love in a haunting melody on the violins. Then, the Princess responds to his adoring declaration with rapid and excited passages, first on solo clarinet and then on solo flute. To a delicate rhythm on side drum and tambourine, the two lovers join in a dance. Toward the end, a solo violin enters as the voice of the storyteller, Scheherezade herself. And all the while, the magic and mystery of the East cast a spell over this ravishing music.

LOVE OF THE SEA

Nikolai Rimsky-Korsakov had two great loves: music and the sea. As a boy, his ambition was to join the navy like his elder brother, and he sailed around the world as a young officer with the Imperial Russian Fleet. He eventually returned home to become Inspector of Naval Bands and professor at the St. Petersburg Conservatory of Music. Later, he devoted as much time as he could to writing music that echoed his lifelong passions.

Rimsky-Korsakov (circled) *as a young cadet in the service of the Imperial Russian Navy.*

A FINE DUET

In 1872, Rimsky Korsakov married Nadezhda Purgold, a gifted pianist. After a prolonged honeymoon in Switzerland and Italy, they enjoyed a highly successful partnership in which she had a great influence on him and was largely responsible for her husband's published piano works.

THE FAMOUS FIVE

Rimsky-Korsakov was the leading member of a group of Russian composers known as "The Five" or "The Mighty Handful." The others were: Mily Balakirev, Alexander Borodin, César Cui, and Modest Mussorgsky. They were all amateurs, in the sense that they came to music from other walks of life. But between them they created a Russian nationalist school of music. As it turned out, Rimsky-Korsakov wrote more music than the rest of them put together.

One of the set designs for the ballet Scheherezade *(above) staged by Diaghilev (right).*

SCHEHEREZADE: THE STORY

The symphonic suite *Scheherezade* is based on the famous collection of stories known as *Tales from the Arabian Nights*. Their legendary author was the Princess or Sultana Scheherezade, whose husband, the Sultan Shahriar, swore to execute each of his new wives after their wedding night because he believed all women to be faithless. Scheherezade fortunately kept postponing her own execution by diverting the Sultan with her wonderful stories, until he finally renounced his terrible vow. The other movements from the work are: "The Sea and Sinbad's Ship," "The Story of Prince Kalendar," and "Festival at Baghdad and Shipwreck."

MASTER OF ORCHESTRATION

Like his fellow countryman Tchaikovsky, Rimsky-Korsakov was a master of orchestration—writing music of vivid descriptive power for a large orchestra. He also wrote a book on how to blend the different sounds we can hear in his own compositions. Rimsky-Korsakov's *Russian Easter Festival Overture* is another of his dazzling orchestral showpieces.

KEY NOTES

A "symphonic suite" is a good way of describing *Scheherezade, since its four episodes, or movements, correspond to the traditional four movements of a symphony.*

JOHANN SEBASTIAN BACH *1685–1750*

Double Violin Concerto in D Minor

BWV 1062: SECOND MOVEMENT

Against the soft background of the string orchestra, the two solo violins blend their voices in the manner of a sublime love duet to create a divinely inspired piece of music. The technical name for this type of composition—weaving two or more melodic parts around each other—is "counterpoint." Johann Sebastian Bach successfully used this technique to create one of the most romantic pieces of music ever written.

POINT AND COUNTERPOINT

The musical term "counterpoint" is from the Latin words *punctus contra punctum*, meaning "point against point," or "note against note." It was first used in the Middle Ages to describe a combination of simultaneously sounding musical lines. An element of counterpoint exists in virtually all music.

KEY NOTES

Bach is renowned as one of the most productive composers of all time, but he was prolific in other areas, too. Twice married, he fathered no less than twenty children!

GAETANO DONIZETTI
1797–1848

L'Elisir
d'amore

UNA FURTIVA LAGRIMA

*I*n the comical opera *L'Elisire d'amore*, "Una furtiva lagrima" is a celebrated, romantic aria. With its sorrowful introduction on the bassoon, the peasant lad Nemorino reflects upon the twists and turns of love as his girlfriend, Adina, sheds *una furtiva lagrima* ("a secret tear"). In actuality, Nemorino is not quite as downcast as he sounds, since he has sealed their fate with a love potion—the *elisir d'amore* of the title.

BEL CANTO

Arias such as *Una furtiva lagrima* are often said to be in the style of *bel canto*. This term, which means "fine singing," refers to the elegant and controlled vocal style that emerged in Italy around the beginning of the 19th century. Donizetti and operatic composer Bellini are two masters of *bel canto*.

UNPROMISING START

Donizetti was born in dire poverty in Bergamo in Northern Italy. He managed to rise from this unpromising background thanks to Johannes Simon Mayr, who directed his musical education and supported him unwaveringly. In 1828, Donizetti married Virginia Vaselli, the daughter of a lawyer in Rome. None of their three children survived infancy, and Virginia's death during a cholera epidemic left him a broken man. In spite of his personal sadness, Donizetti still forged a musical career. But it was cut short by syphilis and the unfortunate composer ended his days half paralyzed and mentally unbalanced.

The house of Johannes Simon Mayr (above), *who helped his young pupil Donizetti rise out of poverty and obscurity.*

BROUGHT BACK TO LIFE

Many of Donizetti's operas were forgotten for a time. Even *L'Elisir d'amore* was neglected for many years until the famous singer Enrico Caruso made an early gramophone recording of "Una furtiva lagrima." The record was an instant hit. Caruso went on to sing the role of Nemorino at New York's Metropolitan Opera in 1904, and *L'Elisir d'amore* was brought back to life.

KEY NOTES

Donizetti wrote sixty-seven operas in under thirty years and dominated Italian opera between the death of Bellini in 1835 and the emergence of Verdi. He wrote comic and serious opera with equal ease.

JOHANNES BRAHMS *1833–1897*

Symphony No.3 in F Major

OPUS 90: THIRD MOVEMENT

*B*rahms is considered a serious-minded composer. But this lovely movement shows that he could be as romantic in mood as Tchaikovsky or Rachmaninov. The main theme, which is heard first on the cellos and later on the solo horn, has a haunting sadness about it, suggesting either a lost love or a love never found.

TRIOS AND THIRDS

The middle part of this movement is known as the trio section. Going back into the history of the symphony, third movements were traditionally modeled on the courtly minuet dance, which originally had a middle section played on a trio of three instruments. So the name stuck, though by the time of Johannes Brahms, it no longer had real meaning.

A LONELY MAN

Brahms *(right)* had a wide circle of friends, but he was in many ways a shy and lonely man, especially when it came to love affairs. He fell in love with Clara Schumann *(right)*, the widow of Robert. But while they were good friends and maintained a close correspondence, it is thought that he never actually pursued her romantically. Of course there were other women who almost certainly would have married him, had Brahms asked them, but he never did and he remained a confirmed bachelor.

A caricature of Brahms on his way to "The Red Hedgehog," the Viennese café where the lonely composer often sought solace.

WEIGHED DOWN

Brahms once said, "You don't know what it is like having that giant always on your back." The "giant" he was speaking of was Beethoven. For years Brahms hesitated before publishing his First Symphony, afraid that people would compare it with Beethoven's nine great ones. In any event, *Symphony No.1* proved a triumph for Brahms, and he wrote his other three symphonies much more easily. For many music lovers, Brahms's four symphonies are the finest group of symphonic works, after those of Beethoven.

KEY NOTES

The celebrated German conductor Hans Richter, a close friend of the composer, called his Symphony No.3 "Brahms's Eroica." Richter was referring to Beethoven's Symphony No.3, which is titled Eroica (or "Heroic Symphony").

GABRIEL FAURÉ 1845–1924

Pelléas et Mélisande

SICILIENNE

This enchanting piece, with its prominent parts for flute and harp, comes from the incidental theater music that Gabriel Fauré wrote for a play, *Pelléas et Mélisande*. The "sicilienne" is the name of an old type of dance or song that probably originated in Sicily. The gentle rippling rhythm here suggests both the charm and innocence of the maidenly Mélisande and her ardent young lover Pelléas *(right)*.

DRAMATIC LOVE

Pelléas et Mélisande is a play by Belgian dramatist Maurice Maeterlinck. Set in a legendary Celtic kingdom by the sea, it is the story of a love triangle and a jealous and tragic murder. The strange and poetic atmosphere of the play made a big impression at the turn of the century. Various composers, such as Schoenberg and Sibelius, wrote music inspired by it, while Debussy's *Pelléas et Mélisande* is one of the greatest operas ever.

KEY NOTES

Fauré originally wrote his "Sicilienne" for cello and piano. However, he liked it so much that he decided to orchestrate it and include it in his incidental music to Pelléas et Mélisande.

SERGEI RACHMANINOV 1873–1943

Piano Concerto No. 2 in C Minor

OPUS 18: SECOND MOVEMENT

The movement opens with a long melody on solo flute to a gentle piano accompaniment that is full of yearning. The music gradually becomes more exhilarating, finally breaking into a flurry of notes—almost like the racing of a lover's heart—before returning to the plaintive melody, now played on violins. The closing bars, or measures, on the piano are more consoling, after the soul-searching mood of the rest of the movement. This is the tender side of love, with some of its pain and melancholy.

Right: *August Rodin's famous sculpture* The Kiss *captures some of the passion of Rachmaninov's most famous piano concerto.*

MOVING TO AMERICA

Sergei Rachmaninov was born in old Tsarist Russia on his large family estate near Novgorod. He studied music at both the St. Petersburg and Moscow conservatories and became the greatest pianist-composer of his generation. In 1909, he toured America, during which time he wrote the Third Piano Concerto. He was well received and was invited to remain in the States. However, he chose to return to Moscow for a few more years. He had already written some of his best works when, at the age of forty-four, the Bolshevik Revolution drove him from his homeland in 1917. Rachmaninov remained in exile for the rest of his life, dividing his time between Europe and America, where he composed and gave concert tours. He never returned to Russia, dying at his home in Beverly Hills, California.

Above: *Sergei Rachmaninov was a devoted husband and father.*

BRIEF ENCOUNTER

The music of the *Piano Concerto No.2* was used in a classic British movie, *Brief Encounter (left)*. Many people still fondly recall this touching love story from fifty years ago, not least because of Rachmaninov's evocative music.

DEEPEST DEPRESSION

 Fellow Russian composer Igor once described Rachmaninov *(right)* as "a six-and-a-half-foot scowl" because he was so tall and was very rarely seen smiling. His melancholy played an important part in how the *Piano Concerto No.2* came to be written. Three years earlier, in 1897, the first performance of Rachmaninov's First Symphony had been a disaster. In the deepest depression and despair, the composer consulted Dr. Nicholas Dahl, a pioneer Moscow hypnotherapist. His therapist succeeded in restoring Rachmaninov's self-confidence, and the result was this most successful and much-loved piano concerto, dedicated to Dr. Dahl.

VIRTUOSO PIANIST

 Part of Rachmaninov's fame and brilliance as a pianist can be attributed to his unusually large hands, with their very long fingers and thumbs. He could stretch his hands and fingers further across the keyboard than practically any other pianist. Much of his own piano music, known for its big chords and rapid, glittering runs up and down the keyboard, echoes this unique physical ability.

KEY NOTES

The piano plays a quiet arpeggio accompaniment in this movement, while other instruments in the orchestra play the melody. The Italian word arpeggio means "in the manner of a harp"—playing the notes of a chord spread out, or one note at a time.

Credits & Acknowledgments

PICTURE CREDITS

Cover /Title and Contents Pages/ IBC: The Image Bank/Romilly Lockyer

AKG London: 3(b), 5, 14, 21(t); Artothek/Josef S. Martin: 12; Bridgeman Art Library, London/Glasgow Museum & Art Gallery: 2; Lauros-Giraudon: 3(tl); Cooley Gallery, Old Lyme, Connecticut: 10; Giraudon/Hotel de Soubise, Paris: 17; A & F Pears Ltd., London: 18; Museum of London: 19(b); Kunsthalle, Hamburg: 20; Haags Gemeentemuseum: 21(b); Giraudon/Private Collection: 23; ET Archive: 16(l); Delaware Art Museum, Samuel and Mary R. Bancroft Memorial, 1935: 4; Robert Harding Picture Library/P. Hawkins: 7(l); Hulton Getty: 19(c), 25(b): Syndication: 25(t); ILN Picture Library: 13(r); Images Colour Library: 6(t) 11(tr); Lebrecht Collection: 7(r), 11(bl & br), 13(l), 15(r), 16(r), 21(b): Karl Pollak: 6(b); Celene Rosen: 19(t); Performing Arts Library/Clive Barda: 9; James McCormick: 8; Roger-Viollet: 3(tr); Ronald Grant Archive/Rank: 24(b); Society for Cultural Relations for the USSR: 15(l), 24(t); Sotheby's Picture Library: 22.

All illustrations and symbols: John See